Sparx

Issue 1

*Anthology of Writing by the
Society of Women Writers Victoria*

First published by Busybird Publishing 2017
Copyright © 2017 remains with the contributors

ISBN 978-1-925585-60-5

Authors: various
Cover image: Kev Howlett
Layout: Busybird Publishing

Editing Committee: Errol Broome, Lynne Santos, Mary Jones, Paula Wilson, Maribel Steel, Blaise van Hecke

Typeset in Palatino 12pt

This anthology is a production of the Society of Women Writers Victoria

The Society is a network linking professional and novice women authors, poets, journalists and general writers accross Australia

www.swwvic.org.au

*The first edition of Sparx is dedicated to Dulcie Stone for
her continued support of the SWWV and her work
in the disability sector.*

Contents

Welcome to the first issue of *Sparx*. This collection of poetry and prose is by members of the Society of Women Writers Victoria and it will entertain and delight you. We all love a good story and we've been telling them for countless generations. It's how we make sense of the world, how we share ideas with each other and entertain ourselves.

The Society of Women Writers was founded in Sydney as a state body in 1925 to welcome women delegates and wives of delegates to the Imperial Press Conference held in Sydney that year. The organisers included the writer, Mary Gilmore, and the journalist, Constance Robertson. In 1970 Margaret Hazzard and a group of women writers in Melbourne formed the Victorian Branch of the Society of Women Writers, which became an incorporated not-for-profit society in 2000. The SWWV Biennial Literary Award was inaugurated in 2001 to celebrate this event. We have sister societies of Women Writers in New South Wales, Queensland, Tasmania and Western Australia.

The group now focuses on linking professional and novice female authors, poets, journalists and general writers across Australia. We aim to draw them together and encourage professional skills through regular conduct of workshops, seminars, conferences, book launches, competitions, this journal and group meetings. Through these activities, the Society encourages women to publish their work.

This publication also includes the three winners from the Margaret Hazzard Short Story Award 2016. This award was established in 1987 to honour Margaret Hazzard and is awarded biennially.

Enjoy!

Blaise van Hecke
President

Mr Brown Jumper

Megan Wallens

Winner of the Margaret Hazzard Short Story Award 2016

I was partly undone by Anne, twice. She was a perfectionist, so in the end I was her unflawed creation. For a while, as I waited in limbo for her hands to rework me, I was ashamed of my useless incompleteness. But for her, it seemed that all the unpicking and unravelling, then the re-casting, counting and re-knitting made my end result worthwhile. She filled me with love and service. Later, when she'd finally cast off my last sleeve, setwn up my pieces and pressed me, I felt truly beautiful and worthy of him. But she was tempting fate.

She thought that through me her knitted-in love would keep him close to her, warm when his nights were lonely and cold. That was at the start. Although she hummed and muttered over my stitches, my myriad rows and extra cable needles, she never once spoke his name in my presence. She wrote her shorthand language for my maze of dense textured patterning in a well-used notebook under 'Brown Jumper, triple cables. WW. May 1968'.

My brown ribbing was simple (P2,K2) with red and orange stripes on size 9 needles, but my body and sleeves were complex. For example, for the start of my front, her notes read 'Change to size 8 needles. Row 1. (P1,K1) 3 times, *P2, "C6F", P2, K7, "C3B", K1 tbl, "C3F", K7, rep from* 3 times, P2, "C6F", P2, (K1,P1) 3 times ...'. With memory in her fingers, she held two large steel needles and added a number of smaller cable ones. They were like giant safety pins to hold my twisted stitches behind or in front of my body as she worked. The cabled lengths slowly spread from her hands, down over her lap in a lava-flow of soft brown merino wool, to eventually evolve into me.

Later, when she was sewing me up, she told Gloria how dull the man was and that she no longer loved him. It was the Boyfriend Curse, she said, a spell cast with the first stitches that gave the knitter time to think and reconsider! It lasted as long as it took to knit a man's jumper. Perhaps he and I were a good match. Being brown, I was dull, too. But I was an intimate expression of her being at that time, and she was delighted with me when we parted.

It took me a while to learn the back story. Long before Anne had designed and created me, she was a competent knitter. By the age of 12 years, she'd learnt everything from her exacting but now sadly deceased mother, whose knitting was flawless. Whenever Anne knitted, she knew in her young heart that Mother's critical eye was observing her work from Above. Accordingly, as she knitted away her sadness and grief, she'd partly unravel a seemingly perfect sleeve, or a front, or a back. That's what happened with me, twice. Gradually it's how I learnt about Anne and her friend Gloria. Like me as I grew, their story gained form and substance.

For instance, I learnt that for five years, Anne had constantly knitted as she travelled by train back and forth to secondary school. This was hundreds of kilometres each way from Dubbo in western New South Wales to Sydney to attend Abbotsleigh girls' boarding school. And how late one January in 1962, when she was 15, Anne met Gloria on the Sydney bound train. Gloria had just embarked on her first 950km journey from Wilcannia to Sydney; she was three years younger, a new boarder at Abbotsleigh. Anne took the younger girl under her wing, became Gloria's mentor. Later, when going home for holidays, they'd travel together on the overnight train as far as Dubbo, share a sleeper. Friends for a reason, friends for a season. But this was long before my time.

The girls lost touch when Anne completed her secondary schooling and disappeared to the next stage of her life. When it was her turn to leave school 3 years later, Gloria decided to take up Nursing as a career. She was accepted into Hornsby and District Hospital, not far from Abbotsleigh, and began her four years' training. She lived in the Nurses' Home on the hospital campus, as did all the other young trainees.

One afternoon in her second year of training, Gloria came off duty exhausted after a heavy day on Rofe Ward, a female medical ward full of elderly women with broken hips and femurs. She went to the Day Room, made a pot of tea. On a whim, she took her tray up to the lounge room, where large worn chairs sat grouped like old friends around scattered coffee tables. And quietly sitting in one of the chairs was a young woman in a dressing gown, stitching up a brown knitted garment. Stitching my front to my back at the shoulders! 'Anne?'

Unknown to Gloria, Anne had completed her training at another Sydney hospital and was now a qualified Registered Nurse, a 'Sister' on permanent night duty, and she too lived in the Nurses' Home. She'd been asleep all day, had just surfaced.

The girls filled in the gaps of their shared but separate stories, as if they were mending moth holes. Anne's fingers flew, and there was a great moment when at last I become whole. Then I was placed to one side. I listened in a lightly folded way and learned something of my destiny. It was obvious by the dismissive way that Gloria fingered my beautiful triple cables and red and orange stripes, that she didn't like me one bit. 'Why on earth this ugly brown? Anyway, who's the jumper for?' she asked.

Anne said, 'My boyfriend. But I've fallen out of love with him. They say one should never knit a jumper for a new boyfriend, it's fatal! You know, the Boyfriend Curse! I thought the wool and style would suit him, and they do, but it's given me a chance to really think. He's a good man, just dull and boring and predictable, no excitement. I've decided that he's not for me. It's over!'

'I've never even had a boyfriend.' replied Gloria, wistfully. Despite her unkind attitude towards me, I felt briefly sorry for her.

'You will! You're only a kid, really. Don't worry. It will happen.' Anne leant over and put her hand on Gloria's knee. She repeated 'It will!'

Soon I waited in pressed perfection wrapped within white tissue paper. We sat inside his green HK Holden. Anne said 'Here, I made this for you!' and she thrust me into his strong warm hands. The paper was ripped off, and I was exposed. I felt the unfamiliar male strength of him as he shook me out and held me up. A deep resonating voice drawled 'Jeeze, Annie! What a beauty. You made this, hey?! I like these red and orange stripes. Ummm, different, aren't they?'

Then he shrugged himself into my body, slid his long arms through my sleeves. I cascaded in strong cabled waves down his back, and he straightened my basque over the top of his hips. He adjusted his white collar and skinny tie over my ribbed neck edge. I enveloped him perfectly, surrounded him with love and warmth just as Anne had intended. And I still didn't know his name when Anne said goodbye to him forever and jumped out of his car.

I moved into his life and out of Anne's. He wore me often in winter for a couple of years, usually when he went to matches with his mates at the Sydney Football Stadium. And then I was packed into a suitcase with other clothes, taken to his mother's house near Canberra. She gently washed me in Lux soap and Eucalyptus Oil, dried me in the sun. She scattered anti-moth flakes on top of me to send away the little wool-eaters. Being nibbled at and made holey by greedy moths was the one thing I became terrified of, especially when I thought of all the love and skill Anne had put into me.

And there I stayed, dry and safe, in the suitcase. Undisturbed.

***

Many years later, I'm woken from my naphthalene hibernation by teary talk. The kind old mother has gone to Heaven, and the man's arrived to clear out her house, ready it for sale. I hear him plead with his unhappy wife in that slow deep resonating voice from way back 'Aww, come on Love! Don't worry. You won't have to do a thing. I'll just take the stuff to Willow Grange and sort it out later.' And I'm carried in the suitcase to a farm house near Leeton in the south, stacked in an office along with myriad boxes of his mother's books, crockery and paintings. And here I slumber for more years, forgotten.

He often works here on the computer or makes business calls. He seems quite successful as a cotton grower with large tracts of irrigated land not far from the Murrumbidgee River. He and his wife have been farming here for 44 years. And I learn that his name is Will Watson. I can't help learning that, because every time he takes a phone call, his voice cheerfully booms 'G'day! This is Will Watson from Willow Grange. How can I help?'

During a wet spell, Will cleans up his office and rediscovers the suitcase. He rediscovers me. I'm removed from the darkness, brought into daylight. The smelly naphthalene flakes are shaken from me. Will inspects me with renewed affection. 'Good ol' Mum, no moth holes! About time I fished you out, Mr. Brown Jumper! Perfectly good and goin' to waste in this cold weather!'

It seems that Will and his wife have been invited to a barbeque on the property next door. New neighbours. As Will wisely says, 'You have to make a good impression the first time, Love. The second time's too late!' so they decide to dress up a bit. The wife goes to town and has her hair done. Their hostess has advised them to wear something really warm 'as we'll be outside albeit with a bonfire!'

'Who on earth says "albeit"?' laughs Will 'but we better rug up, eh Love'. And this is when I fully re-enter the world.

Will comes into his office, takes me from the hanger behind the door and pulls me on. I fear that I'll be too small for him; after all, it's over 40 years since Anne made me for him. To our astonishment, I still fit him perfectly. My mossy cables ripple down over his slim body, his arms slide into my sleeves as they did so long ago, my V-shaped neckline neatly holds the collar of his new R M Williams shirt. 'Hurry up, Will! I'm sick and tired of waiting. It's cold.' calls his wife.

Will shuts the door, walks out towards the shed, where she's waiting under the outside light beside the truck. She's wearing a long red coat, knee high boots, and her back is turned to us. Bill says 'What d'ya think, Glory Love? It still fits!'

She turns under the light. It's Gloria! I instantly recognise her, as she does me! As she sees Will wearing me, she staggers backwards against the truck, stares at us in disbelief. She gasps and points 'Where'd that horrible brown thing come from?'

Bill says with his big bland smile 'It's been in the old suitcase since before Mum died. Remember when we cleared out her house, an' you didn't want to do it? M'old girlfriend made it for me years before you and I met. I could never chuck it out; look at the wonderful stitchin'. She was a good woman, just dull and boring, predictable, no excitement, and always bloody knittin'! Come on, Glory Love, get yerself in the truck!'

And off we go, bouncing through the frosty night down the track to the gate.

Ms Writer's Block

Non-fiction Group

This was created by a SWWV collective writing challenge: 'How to get beyond writer's block.'

Dear Ms Writers Block,
It's not you, it's me, and I have to say good-bye to you once and for all.

I know that to write, I must do several things:
I promise faithfully to write for at least one hour every morning.

I must not look at my emails, and I must turn off all devices to limit distractions.

I will sit down in my writing space and challenge myself to write ... something ... anything ... until the muse appears.

And if she doesn't?

I can sit outside where the sounds of nature will help clear my mind, where I can take inspiration from the world outside to inspire my rich inner world of observation.

I know that scribbling down any words on a blank page can be the source of thought – allowing my creative mind to go down those rabbit holes. I have learned to allow myself to follow these thoughts, I never know what I'll uncover there that will spark ideas for my next narrative.

Hmm. And if that doesn't work?

I will close my eyes to observe with my other senses, to perceive other aspects of the world around me – what can I hear? What can I smell? I will ask myself, does this sensory feeling hold a deeper memory, can I recall a time when...

If story ideas still elude me, then I will practise F.R.E.E writing – Fast, Raw, Exact and Easy. I will write like the clappers for 10 minutes with NO editing in mind, without the writer's critic looking over my shoulder – I will use this time to write and write. Within this process, I may find a seed-thought to begin a new story. And of course, I must never forget to have a notebook nearby because if I don't, that minxy muse will strike when there is no way of capturing her inspired thoughts – especially in the middle of the night.

Return to Athens

Dulcie Stone

'You who know sorrow, beware its darker legacy – despair. For despair, unlike sorrow, locks its door to hope.' – Artemis Dionesius.

My eyes feast on the words. No need to pen them, no need to memorise. Long-etched into my brain, they are my essence; my mind, my heart, my soul, my spirit. This fragment of fragile parchment, one of the randomly selected few suggested by the custodian on my initial visit, is now as familiar as my next breath. Randomly selected? An accident of time and place and opportunity? Or Fate?

I have come from the New World to the Old and here in Athens, in this library of the ancients, I have found myself. Ah, the words! Yes, despair. I know you. I have tasted the cup of sorrow, drunk from its depths, drained it and am condemned to its cruel legacy. Yes, despair. You I truly know. You are my companion, my mentor and my torment, my destiny and my prison.

I beckon the custodian.

Bleakly formal, he arrives. 'How may I help, Sir?'

Careful not to inadvertently touch it, I indicate the precious parchment. 'I've finished.'

'You are leaving early.' A disinterested statement of evident fact.

'Today. Yes.'

He does not immediately leave.

I parrot the anticipated. 'Thank you for your assistance.'

'It is my pleasure, Sir.' He hesitates, and asks: 'I have a question, if I may?'

'Of course.'

'You read Artemis Dionesius.' Another statement of the evident. 'You read him with ease.'

'My father schooled me in the philosophers.'

My great-grandfather's faded daguerreotype on our mantlepiece was an omnipresent childhood companion. Child, adolescent, and adult – always the likeness of the ageing sage for whom I was named watched over me. My father talked of him often, a wise man who knew things I would never need to know.

The custodian re-encases the faded script. 'You are of the Diaspora?'

'My father left reluctantly, after the war. I sometimes think he left his spirit here.'

'Our parents confronted difficult choices.' His hushed feet follow to the tall front doors. 'We will see you tomorrow?'

I do not respond, cannot.

I turn from his shadowed face, step into the midday traffic. The vicious sun, momentarily escaping the ubiquitous smog, assaults my eyes.

A taxi waits. 'Where to, Sir?'

'The Madelaine. You know it?'

He slips into the lazy noon traffic. Of course he knows it. Five-star luxury. A substantial tip anticipated.

Artemis Dionesius? Who were you? Were you too without hope? How is it that I have been led to you? Why?

Long distanced in time and place, I am Greek forever. Young son of a new adventure. Fast cars and sleek machines, gadgetry and opportunism, corruption and ambition, wealth and power. Shallow values and elastic morality. Young man in a young world. Schooled in pragmatic schools yet – unwittingly – forever Greek.

Today's child grown to today's man, heeding not my father's legacy of the ancients – nor anticipating the darkness of my condemned soul. Until she left.

Despair, I know you.

White as untouched snow her hand slips from mine and she is gone. Heart of my heart, breath of my breath, she takes with her our unborn child. Impotent, I am condemned to watch them leave. No gadgetry, no trickery of today's science, no fiscal miracle nor magical potion to stay Fate's incorruptible hand. As it ever was, so it now still is.

'Return to your roots, my son.' My immigrant father, with his last breath, spoke in the beloved tongue of his childhood. 'Return to Athens.'

They are together, these three – wife and child and father. With my long-gone mother, they are under the tall gums and the high skies and the glistening southern stars. My life, they lie entombed and silent.

Despair knows not hope, nor do I.

The taxi slips to the kerb, accepts its due, and slides away into the midday traffic. The five-star atrium is somnolent and dim; obsequious feet silent on lush carpets, muted voices formally greeting.

The lift glides to the highest floor, to the unfamiliar hushed passageways. I unlock the door. A room with a bath. A room with a bath and steaming hot water. Preparations complete, I turn on the taps.

Cold water from the cold tap. From the hot tap, cold. The bath fills. Still, no warmth.

No hot water! Only hot water will hasten this final act. The letting of blood, long planned, long considered. To watch my slow blood flow from me, as I watched hers flow from her. No other way is appropriate.

Tourists touring, management economising; no hot water in the noon-time empty rooms. Doomed to wait, I fall onto the lonely bed.

The jangling telephone blasts.

Not to answer. Never to answer.

The telephone falls silent, acquiescent accessory to my determination.

I doze, and dream unwelcome dreams.

The re-awakened jangle interrupts. Do not answer.

The unwelcome dreams threaten. The phone persists.

Her voice is unfamiliar. 'Mr Kalaris?'

'What do you want?' Impatience dismisses courtesy.

'I'm interrupting.' Her disapproval communicates itself. 'Can I call later?'

'It's not convenient.' I prepare to replace the receiver. 'Do not...'

'Peter,' she interrupts. 'I've been asked to contact you.'

Curiosity stays my hand. 'Do I know you?'

'We have not met.' Her voice is melodious. Her English, though immaculate, is rich with the nuances of Greece. 'I was hoping to meet you.'

How to respond? Why?

'I know your sister,' she continues. 'I know you probably want to be alone. Your sister ...'

'You've come here from Melbourne?'

'Not recently. Tula corresponds. She told me you'd be here. She suggested I show you around.'

'Ah...' Of course. Tula would be worrying about her young brother sulking off to Greece. The unknown woman with the silky voice has been enlisted to rescue me from what my sister might fear. What does she fear? She knows me, my desolation.

'I am free later this week,' she adds.

'Thank you.' Civility replies. 'Tula means well.'

'I understand. You don't want a guide.' Her tone is gentle, even comforting, or would have been had it not touched death.

It impacts as uneasily as a funereal anthem. 'I'm sorry,' I murmur. 'I intend no discourtesy.'

'Of course, Peter. I should not intrude on your grief. Tula means well, as you say.' The line dies.

Not reconnecting the telephone, I sink back onto the disturbed sheets. The waiting will end. Before evening, the waiting will end.

But the intrusion itches. A minute discord, it requires attention. I get up, drink an undiluted whisky, warm and medicinal. My awakened mind grows increasingly restless. Frustrated, I dress, cover my unclear head with a broad straw sunhat, and leave the building.

A taxi waits.

'Where to, Sir?'

'The Necropolis, if you please.' My heart pounds. I do not want to do this.

Phlegmatic, he slips into the accelerating mid-afternoon traffic.

The cemetery is on the outskirts. The pencil-thin cypresses stand gloomy watch, the smog-blighted birds pant laboured breath, the weed-bound graves wither. And the nearby streets scream from another planet.

I walk between the crumpled headstones and for an unanticipated second time squat beside the grave of my great-grandfather.

That first afternoon, I'd come to sit with him, to heed my dead father's words, to touch our roots, and to weep for yesterdays that will never know tomorrows. Until harrowing memories of more personal cemeteries, augmented by distress at the grave's unkempt desolation, had won the day. I'd left, to visit the museum my father had lauded, and to prepare today's mid-day conclusion.

Preparations complete, resolution unwavering, deviating only when the telephone's untimely interference had demanded attention. It still does. Because here I am. Is Fate's voice whispering? Is there unplumbed meaning here?

My great-grandfather's name, though blurred by time and rain and wind and sun and bird droppings, is faintly legible – Petro Georgio Kalaris. The weather-worn dates are barely decipherable.

An insignificant distraction. My father has imprinted them as deftly as has the headstone's Athenic mason.

I read again my great-grandfather's name, the dates, the clichéd formalities that are helplessly surrendering to the ruthless brambles. Too late, I regret this final illogically impulsive pilgrimage. Pain sears. There will be another taxi. Waiting, as they do.

And yet…?

My father's spirit prompts. Have I missed something? What is the message of the ill-timed telephone intrusion?

Careless of consequences, curiosity attacks the dense brambles. Ten minutes of sweating labour reveals what has been long hidden. As veils from the body of a beautiful woman, the centuries peel away, and once more I read: *'You who know sorrow, beware its darker legacy – despair. For despair, unlike sorrow, locks its door to hope.' Artemis Dionesius.*

The words from the ancient parchment, the words that are my essence, are on my great-grandfather's grave. I should have known.

My heart stops. A revelation of time and place and itching disquiet. Chance? Or Fate? My father, and his, would say Fate. However I am a man of reason, a modern man. Therefore reason concludes that my father instilled them long ago. That I am here, not at Fate's beckoning, but because of lessons learned as a child.

The hotel room waits, must wait.

My torn hands attack the remaining stubborn brambles, and the grave's last imprisoned message is released.

'Therefore consider love. Honour love.' Petro Georgio Kalaris.

My great-grandfather, for whom I am named, has ordered an addendum. The words of an unknown, whose grave is dying, modify the message of the revered sage.

Did my father know? These words are not in my memory. Unlike the words of the sage, they ring no childhood bells. They are new.

I sit beside his headstone, my inflexible timetable in jeopardy. The sky becomes red-hazed, the distant traffic hysterical. My great-grandfather's words are irresistibly provocative. Have I considered love? Does my inflexible intent honour love? Have I honoured love! The cemetery is sanctuary, the grave hypnotic...

A lone crow's eerie caw breaks the spell.

I retrace my steps between the weed-bound tombs and the crumpled headstones.

A taxi waits, as they do. 'Where to, Sir?'

'The Madelaine. You know it?'

The evening sun falls behind the Parthenon. The legacy of the ancients lives on. The revered philosophers still speak in the hushed museums.

My room is bleak. I test the taps. The water, hot and steaming, is no longer important. I call long distance: 'Tula?'

Her voice is clear and filled with love. 'I was worried...'

'I'm sorry. I should not have left as I did.'

'Pete? Are you all right?'

'I'll let you know when I'm finished here.' My great-grandfather's grave must be restored.

'Are you sure you're all right!'

'I have a job to do. I'll keep in touch.' The brambles will be rooted out, the head stone rejuvenated, the inscriptions preserved. And his message will be recorded. Perhaps to join the treasured parchments in the museum?

'You're starting work there?'

'In a way.'

'Please come home,' she frets. 'We worry about you.'

'I'll phone every day,' I promise. 'Okay?'

'Okay. We miss you Pete. Take care.'

My tears fall silently, unheard and un-witnessed.

I cut the line, but not the connection.

Tula loves.

And I love.

Reflections

Tricia Veale

Gum trees reflect glisten in early morning lake
I'm watching from the bank for a Platypus
then one surfaces floating in expanding rings
duck-bill forward eyes shining upwards
suddenly he dives back into waterscapes
air bubbles pop to the surface travelling
following the underwater swim down
then he appears again floating breathing
long tail duck feet slowly supporting

a Willy Wagtail chitters pirouettes
balancing fluttering on a floating branch
suddenly a large fish flops upwards splash
large rippling rings and Moorhens jump run
Ducks Coots jerkily swim away downstream
perky Purple Swamp Hen paces the river bank
then a Spoonbill flies past ... twig in beak
landing in the canopy of a spotted gum
building a nest so precariously balanced

many people walk this track and see
the wonders of nature that surround
encompass this garden of natural woodland
hear the bird calls cackling Kookaburras
the shimmering reflections on beautiful lake
flow on swiftly moving to the un-Broken River.

The Blue Beanie

Razmi Wahab

The blue beanie on her head
A hidden story, not a fashion statement.
She was smiling, she was chatting
Last meeting for the year
I will have a little chat with her
But first, this person next to me is saying something
And the time passed and I had to catch the train
I thought about the blue beanie
Hair loss, like friends I have seen fighting cancer
Bright bandanas to lift the spirit
And she had a blue beanie with a story I did not know.
Next meeting, next year I will have a chat with her
I was sure
Death notice does not lie
That is the story of the blue beanie.

Mumbai to Kolkata

Lynne Santos

Chatrapati Shivaji Terminus, also known as Victoria Terminus, is the main train station in Mumbai. Its monumental buttresses, turrets, domes, gargoyles and stained glass windows reflect an eclectic fusion of British, Hindu and Islamic architecture. My journey of over two thousand kilometres across India, from Mumbai on the west coast to Kolkata near the eastern border with Bangladesh, began here. I manoeuvred my way through a teeming mass of pedestrians, buses, taxis, rickshaws, street vendors, motorbikes, cows, bicycles and carts towards the entrance.

Inside the terminus was just as crowded. Two and a half million people pass through the station every day, an entire population on the move. Suspended from the lofty ceiling the Arrival and Departure boards, lit up like constellations, displayed destinations, times and platforms in Hindi and English. As I searched the boards for my train a voice asked, 'Madam, where are you going?'

I turned and a luggage wallah was standing next to me. 'Kolkata.'

'Come.' He heaved my suitcase onto his head and strode through the crowds, beckoning me to keep up. As he delivered me to the right platform, he glanced at my ticket and immediately found the carriage, seat and a place for my case. He held out his hand for payment, nodded and disappeared into the throng.

All through the train a brigade of luggage wallahs were busy re-arranging bags and belongings on overhead racks and under seats to squeeze in even more. Nimble and efficient, they created space where I could see only congestion.

Around me families and friends said their last goodbyes with tears, smiles and waves, the universal language of separation. The engine lurched forward, then stalled as if overwhelmed by the long line of carriages behind it. It surged again, its iron wheels screeching, and pulled away from the platform.

The train trundled past colonial-era edifices of the British Raj, solid on their rock-of-ages foundations: the University of Mumbai, the High Court, St. Thomas's Cathedral. It passed through suburbs of high-rise apartments, their barren uniformity relieved by temples, mosques, bazaars and markets, then the slums, stretching in a vast sprawl. These shanty-towns of concrete blocks and corrugated iron shacks, alleys and open sewers are home to sixty percent of the city's population. Families have lived here for generations and small textile factories, potteries, tanneries, distilleries and plastics recycling businesses thrive. After two hours of slow passage, the train finally left the megalopolis of Mumbai behind.

As I looked out of my open window, hour after hour, India came to me, rolling out its landscapes, displaying its towns and granting glimpses of its villages in a long, continuous panorama: forests in filtered light, tribes of monkeys, temples dedicated to lotus-eyed gods, chlorophyll green rice paddies, clusters of mud huts camouflaged amongst mango trees, crumbling forts, cool climate hill stations, slow, brown rivers, women in jewel-bright saris harvesting fields of grain, abandoned palaces, children flying plastic bag kites, makeshift cricket games in side streets, farmers perched on overloaded ox carts, sacred cows wandering wherever they pleased.

But there was another journey beside this one through landscape; it was the journey inside the train. The two accompanied each other like parallel railway tracks.

Passengers soon formed groups to chat or play cards, spread

out on berths where there was more room, put their feet up. Kids ran up and down the aisle and women nursed babies. The tea wallah came through regularly with his urn of sweet, milky tea and his throaty call, "Chai, chai chai."

We stopped at a small station in a flatland of stubbled fields. We were in the heartland of Maharashtra. Chaff and dust blew into the train. I heard distant music, folk music, growing louder and more distinct until a band of itinerant musicians entered our carriage. They wore the dust of the surrounding country, their faces were deeply weathered by sun and wind and their eyes showed the harshness of their lives. They sang their age-old songs in strong, loud voices and played simple, traditional instruments. They passed a cap around and then moved on like a tribe of nomads.

A small boy climbed onto my berth and opened his school exercise book. He showed me the English words he was learning to spell: HOUSE FAMILY GRANMOTHER. I corrected this last word and then we played noughts and crosses until the train pulled into a large town. Vendors thrust cold drinks and plastic bags of sliced fruit through the windows. We re-arranged our seating to accommodate more passengers and luggage. The train shunted forward and we had just re-settled when a group of Hijras, a caste of transvestites and eunuchs, invaded. They smiled coquettishly, fluttering their lashes and jangling their bangles. Their long plaits swung and heavy perfume thickened the air. They marched up to the men, clapping their hands loudly in their faces and demanding baksheesh, or else! One man was foolish enough to deny them so they surrounded him and raised the hems of their saris, higher and higher, threatening to reveal... It was only a matter of centimetres before his resolve collapsed. With laughter, amorous cries and provocative gestures they left us, a flock of bright birds of prey.

Meanwhile the landscape continued to slide past my window, a silent and changing backdrop. The dinner wallah made his round, delivering thalis of vegetable curry, dhal, raita, rice and chapattis; some of the women brought out their own hampers of home-cooked meals in metal tiffins. Aromas spiced the air. I watched in awe as even the children chewed raw or pickled chillies with their meal. Fluorescent lights blinked on, the sun set in a flare of colours and the first, faint stars began to populate the sky. Occasionally, the bright, electric lights of towns and the soft lamplights of villages illuminated the darkness. Middle and upper bunks were pulled down and children were tucked up under a blanket or shawl.

Sitting opposite me a retired teacher, Professor Karwah, with whom I'd been discussing the Hindu belief in reincarnation, offered to read my palm. 'You will travel, so much travel, but you'll come back to India many times.' He traced my lifeline with his index finger. 'And you will live until you are eighty-eight years old.'

I was pleased with this prospect of longevity. 'Then I'll be reborn?'

He shrugged. 'If God wills it.'

I climbed up to my top bunk and stretched out under my sheet to share the privacy and intimacy of sleep with strangers, to dream in the company of others. Gently jostled by the motion of the train and lulled by the sighs, mutters and deep breathing around me, I too fell asleep. On into the night we travelled.

*****

The chai wallah woke us with his early morning cry. We packed up our bunks and took turns to wash and brush our teeth in the sinks located in the two squat toilets at either end of our carriage. Women braided their hair, adjusted the folds of their saris and sat straight-backed and elegant.

By now the rhythmic motion of the train was internal, like my own pulse. The journey seemed to have had no beginning and would have no end and I was happy to go on this never-ending ride.

The train made its first stop for the day. I jumped out and bought a fried egg sandwich, spiced with cayenne pepper, from one of the crowded food stalls. The train jolted forward and I jumped back on.

A flicker of movement caught the corner of my eye. A young boy somersaulted, back flipped and cartwheeled down the aisle. Two others followed close behind. They grabbed whatever coins we held out before springing and tumbling into the next carriage.

'Tickets, tickets!' An inspector, in a grubby uniform, appeared in the doorway.

I pulled my ticket out of my pocket. He punched a hole in it and scribbled something on his list.

'Where are you from?'

'Australia.'

'Oh, cricket. Shane Warne, Ricky Ponting!'

It's is the common response I receive in this cricket-mad country.

'But Sachin Tundulkar is the best.'

He gave the characteristic head wag that signals acquiescence. 'But Aussie team is number one. Ozzie, ozzie, ozzie, oy oy oy.' He chuckled and moved on. 'Calcutta in one hour,' he called back to me.

One hour? I had lost my sense of clock-time. This journey had been marked not by hours but by the irregular stops at stations. Instead of the ticking of a clock there'd been the clackety clack of train wheels.

A new group of visitors appeared, the disabled, many crippled by polio. They crawled on twisted limbs along the floor of the aisle and under the berths, sweeping up our rubbish with rags and flaps of cardboard for a few rupees.

Everyone was stirring, gathering their luggage, bundles, bags and children in preparation for a mass exodus from the train. We crossed Howrah Bridge, seven hundred and five metres of steel cantilevers. Below us was the Hooghly River. At this time, dusk, devotees were bathing with their hands joined in prayer and making offerings of marigolds and incense to its life-giving waters. The train approached Howrah station with its sturdy towers and broad facade of arches. We crowded into the aisle. With a last metallic groan the wheels ground to a stop. We pushed forwards towards the doorways and immediately we were replaced by a legion of destitute street kids who scavenged for bottles of water, food scraps and whatever other treasures we may have left behind.

I walked, dazed, along the platform that seemed to be moving under my feet. My epic train journey was over. For thirty-six hours I'd experienced constant movement and change, the pleasures of being in transit. But now I had arrived.

Going Home

Paula Wilson

'I'm going home.'

'Billy we ain't got no home that's why we're here.' Sam pulled the rough blanket over his shoulder.

'D ... do so.'

Sam could hear movement in the bed next to him. 'You ain't crying?' he asked.

'Nah. Course not.' There was more movement.

'Good. You don't wanna be crying around here,' Sam whispered.

'Doesn't matter, I'm going home.'

Sam sighed, 'I keeps telling you we don't have no home. Kids like us don't have homes.'

'Do so,' Billy said again. 'Ma said it was for a couple of weeks. While she sorted her head. A holiday.'

'Some holiday.' Sam rolled over on his side to face Billy. 'You been here three months now.'

'Nah, eleven weeks and five days.'

'Get used to it, kid. We're here till they kick us out at fourteen. Then we goes to work at the brick works.'

'Well I ain't working at no brick works,' Billy said.

'It's there or the tannery. That's where we all end up.'

'I'm leaving tomorrow.'

Sam leant up on his elbow facing Billy.

'Gotta get home for Walter's birthday,' Billy continued.

'Who's Walter?' Sam asked.

'Me brother. He's ten on Sunday.'

'Didn't know you had any brothers.'

'I got three brothers and two sisters.' Sam heard Billy take a deep breath. 'Walter and me are twins.'

'So how come you're here?'

'Dunno. I heard them saying something about Ma had enough. Said she needed a break.'

Sam lay quiet for a while staring at the ceiling. He thought Billy had gone to sleep so rolled on his side and curled into a ball. Before he could close his eyes he heard a sob. This time he didn't ask Billy if he was crying, but said, 'What's home like Billy?'

'You'd love it. Us boys share a bedroom but it ain't nothing like here. We have bunks not rows of beds. And soft blankets. We got pictures on the walls too. We got a big back yard where Dad grows vegetables and there's fruit trees. We all play on the street.'

'Ain't that dangerous?' Sam had never played on the street. He had never played anywhere but behind the walls surrounding the grounds. Except when they snuck out to explore the woods on the other side.

'Nah,' Billy said.

'So what do you play?'

'Footy. Cricket. But we got in a whole pile of trouble last time we played 'cause I hit a sixer and broke Mrs Braxton's window.' Billy laughed. 'You shoulda seen her come running out. She was shaking her washing stick and chased us all the way down the street.' Billy went silent.

'Did you have to pay?'

'Nah they brought me here two days later.' Billy did not say any more.

Sam lay on his back, hands behind his head. Home. Home sounded good. He thought maybe he would like to try it.

***

Sam finished making his bed. He looked up to see Billy struggling to do the corners like they were supposed to be done. If Billy did not get it right he would be in a whole lot of trouble again. Sam went over and started on the opposite corner to Billy.

'So what time are you going?' Sam snapped his corner into position and tucked the sheet and blanket under the mattress.

'Tonight. After everyone's asleep,' Billy said without looking up.

'Can I come?'

Billy stopped doing his corner and stared at Sam. 'You wanna come?'

'Yeah. Ain't had no home but here. Wouldn't mind trying a real home.'

Billy thought about it for a full half second. 'Sure.'

****

Eleven-thirty. The whole building was asleep. Except for Sam and Billy. They dropped two pillowcases, stuffed with their possessions, from the dormitory window. There was a soft thud as they hit the ground. The boys climbed through the window and lowered themselves down. They slung the pillowcases over their shoulders and ran away from the building. Light rain drizzled down on them as they made their way from shrub to tree, tree to shrub.

At the drystone wall that surrounded the grounds they stopped and crouched low. Sam looked back at the great bluestone building. It loomed a dark shadow in the night. No light shone from any of the windows.

Billy nodded and whispered, 'Okay, let's do this.'

They both stood and threw their pillowcases on top of the wall. As Sam went to pull himself up a dark shadow emerged from an overhanging tree and swooped towards them. He dropped flat out on the ground and buried his face in wet grass.

'Hooo Hooo Hooo.' An owl. Sam looked at Billy who pulled

his head out of the grass and gave him a big grin. They got back to their feet, clambered up the wall and sat with their legs dangling over the edge.

'Well this is it,' Sam said.

'We're going home, we're going home.' Billy grabbed his pillowcase and jumped down into long grass.

Sam twisted around to look at the building. He searched for the window to his dormitory. Second floor, five from the right, but the windows had merged with the darkness of the bluestones and he could only guess where it was. He had been in that room since ... since forever. He could not remember living anywhere else. The other kids would wake and he would be gone; he had been with most of them for forever too.

'You coming?' Billy called.

'Yeah.' He went to drop the pillowcase holding his possessions, his life. 'Nah.'

Billy stared up at him.

'Don't think I will.'

'Oh.'

Sam could hardly hear him. 'It's okay Billy, you go. Go home.'

Billy tapped his forehead with two fingers. Sam returned the salute as Billy turned and ran towards the woods. Sam sat on the wall as the drizzle turned to rain. He watched Billy disappear into the trees then swung his legs round, jumped off the wall and strode across the grounds, back home.

The Flood

Blaise van Hecke

An excerpt from the upcoming memoir, *The Road to Tralfamadore is Bathed in River Water.*

The wind rattles the corrugated iron roofing. The straight ghost gum at the back of the house sways, dropping branches that make a whipping crack as they hit the earth. Relentless rain batters at the tin for hours and I chant a mantra over and over *please stop raining, please stop raining.* It continues for days on end and we battle to light the fire even with the use of kero, its blue hued liquid fizzing against the damp kindling.

Endless hours turn to days. Wet, wet, wet. We watch the river, holding our breath, and then it rises. Rises like a monster awakening from slumber. Water covers the rocks and trees and creeps steadily upwards, towards the house. Please stop raining, please stop raining.

We speculate about whether the water has ever covered our little hill, suck in our breath and marvel at the speed and power of the water as whole trees sail past – roots and all – some stopping at our crossing downstream and creating a new bridge for us to use to cross the river or as a diving jetty – a new place to play.

The river is swollen, surly and churned up with mud and debris, sometimes even a cow, a car part or some roofing iron.

If it stops raining, the river will drain away into the sea in as many days as it came. Please stop raining, please stop raining. If it doesn't stop raining then we are stranded on our little island bound by the river on one side and the creek on the other. The only way out is along the saddle out the back, a narrow ridge now made narrower by the rising waters on either side. Please stop raining, please stop raining.

And if it doesn't stop raining we will run out of food because there is only so much to be picked from the garden in winter. Please stop raining, please stop raining.

A meeting is held. I don't know how word gets to us. There is always someone who will travel around the bush regardless of the weather, regardless of the situation. In my minds-eye it's Maddy but I don't know for sure. But a meeting happens and the majority agree that everyone should take what they can and head out to town.

We are adventurers on a quest carrying bundles of clothes on our backs. There are children, babies and dogs of all shapes and sizes. Some are good at being on an adventure. Others grizzle and want to be carried. It is a slow trek along the bush tracks, then out onto the road. Wet, slippery and muddy. The tears from heaven are finished so my need for chanting is over but the water still rises in the river as our convoy trudges along the rain-soaked earth.

At the first river crossing we stand to assess the situation. The roiling brown water is angry, churning, thrashing at the riverbank on both sides. The speed of it seems immense and we wonder if we can cross, even with the rope tied to a tree on both sides of the river.

We take it in turns to cross. The taller, stronger people take bundles and kids on their heads until we are all safely on the other side. It's a long day, this adventure, and we repeat the river crossing four more times. It takes six hours to walk to the Yowrie Post Office where we keep our car. Mama has promised us fish and chips at the co-op in Bermie. We lick our lips at the thought of the greasy saltiness then fall asleep as soon as we get in the car to drive from Yowrie to Bermagui. We take our fish and chips to Alan's house up on the hill looking over the sea. It's not raining here so we feel like we are in another country even though the river house is just over there, over the mountain and down in the valley.

A Dog, a Hat and a Moneybox

Judith A Green

Second place in the Margaret Hazzard Short Story Award 2016

'There ya go sonny.' A large, anonymous tin thuds onto the counter, belching dust. A jagged slit in the lid confirms it is a homemade moneybox.

'Ya ain't gonna charge me fer countin' it are ya?' Two weather-beaten hands clutch the tin.

Five minutes to closing. Friday afternoon.

'Ya ain't gonna charge me fer countin it are ya?' he repeats. 'The last bloke said he would. Took it home with me again. Bloody cheek. Chargin' a bloke to count his money. I'm old, not senile.'

I shake my head. The hands loosen pushing the tin towards me. I tip some of the coins onto the counter spreading them thinly.

'Got a bit a' old stuff in there still. Had a bit of a tidy up when me missus died. Amazin' what ya find at the back of the cupboard. What ya forgot ya had. It's all money, ain't it?'

I nod, segregating a few pennies and shillings.

'Thought a' sellin' it to a collecta. You know, them that keep old coins. Reckon its worth much?'

'Depends on the year. Some years are worth quite a deal.'

'Ya know what years they are?'

'No. Sorry.'

'A well. Don't know any collectas anyways. Probly charge me to look at it.'

He pushes a misshapen hat aside, rubs a balding head, returning the hat to position.

'How long ya reckon it'll take ya to count all this?'

I tip again.

'Not sure.'

'Must be lonely workin' in a bank all by yerself. But at least we still gotta Bank. Not like some places.'

'There are other staff – out back.'

The old man inspects the piles of coins accumulating on the counter.

'Sure they're all the same? Look diffrent to me.'

I recount.

'Yes, all the same value.'

'Ever worried about gettin' robbed?'

'Not really.'

I keep counting.

'Got robbed a few years back. When me boys were little tackers. Come home from school fulla the story. Cleaned tha Bank out.'

I stop counting.

'Coupla blokes come into tha Bank at lunchtime when tha young bloke was on by himself. Everyone used to go home fer lunch in them days and all the shops shut, yer see. 'Cept the Bank, they left the young bloke on by himself.'

I nod.

He pauses.

'Come in tha back door. Yeah, come in tha back door. Come and gone before anybody knew. Never did catch the blokes, or get tha money back.'

I resume counting.

'Got ya back door locked sonny?'

I nod.

'Good. Don't want no burglars comin' in while ya countin' me money.'

He looks at the clock.

'Past ya closin' time sonny.'

I check the time.

'Want me ta lock tha door sonny?'

'Thank you.'

'Mind if I bring me dog inside sonny. Gettin' a bit hot out there now. The sun hits this side of the street this time a' day. He's a clean dog sonny.'

'It's okay. There are no other customers.'

'Thanks sonny. That other bloke wouldna let me dog in. Said only guide dogs coulda come in. Fancy bringin' ya money to a bank when ya can't see 'em count it. Not that I think ya'd cheat me sonny. I don't mean you.'

I smile.

He opens the door, whistles, closes the door and turns the snib.

'That all ya lock it with sonny?'

'There is other security when we leave at night.'

'Don't want no one distractin' ya while ya count me money.'

I smile.

'Thank you.'

A black and white kelpie sits beside the old man.

'Rover. That's me dog's name. Rover.'

I salute the dog. A bushy, fox-like tail pounds the floor.

'How's it goin' sonny?'

I tip again.

'Did you know this was here?'

I hand him a small diamond ring.

'Gee, I'd forgotten about that.' He polishes the stone on his shirt. 'I'd forgotten about puttin' that there.'

I continue counting in the silence.

'Belonged to tha' missus, sonny. Belonged to the missus. Put it in there the day she died. Hid it from her sister ya know.'

He polishes it again. I look at the old man. The ring sparkles in the palm of his hand

'Yeah the missus's sister was a fair magpie. Collect anythin' she could. So I hid it in the tin. Buried the missus with her weddin' ring though. Never left her finger from the day we married.'

I watch the old man.

'Got a missus sonny?'

I shake my head.

'Plenty a' time yet sonny, plenty a' time yet. But when ya find the right one treat her right.'

I nod and resume counting.

'Been dead ten years now. Seems like yesterdy.'

The coins clink in the silence.

The old man knots the ring in the corner of a grey hankie pushing it deep into a trouser pocket.

I tip again.

'Forgot about them notes.'

I straighten out five, one hundred dollar notes.

'Me daughter sends 'em to me. Tells me to buy some new clothes. What's tha matta with this lot?'

He surveys the scuffed boots, faded trousers and shirt.

'Buy a new hat me daughter says. A new hat. Me dog wouldna know me if I bought a new hat. Wouldya boy?'

The dog's tail thumps.

'She bought me a new hat once.'

He grins as I look up.

'Bought me this new hat with a string and wooden bead to draw it up tight under me chin. Strangle a guy it could.' His hands clutch his throat.

'You need to keep the sun off your face and neck Dad, she

says. Me old hat does that I say. You don't want people to think you are destitute Dad, she says. How long have you had that hat? A good time I say. A good time. When I bought that tractor from old Fred. I bought it then. Had to buy one. Lost tha other one drivin' the tractor home in the storm. That long she says, that long. Yeah been a good hat I told her. Been a good hat.'

He takes a breath.

'Perhaps it is time to lay it to rest Dad, she says. It has been a good hat, let it rest now. Now girlie I say, don't treat me like no kid.' He wags his finger as he talks. 'This hat's like me. Doesn't look as good as it used to, but it ain't dead yet and neither am I.'

I grin as I count.

'Anyways next time she comes she brings this hat. Big straw thing with this rope and bead to hold it on me head. Just try it for me Dad, just try it. You could wear it to town to do the shopping and keep the other for around the farm Your old hat would last longer for you then.'

I laugh out loud.

'I'm old sonny, not senile. Could see through her little scheme straight away.

But she's a good girl so I put this hat on me 'ead. I'll wear it in goin' around the sheep I told her. Okay, Dad, she says. I'll come with you.'

I keep counting.

'Anyways walk out tha door and tha dog starts. Backs away from me barking fit to wake the dead. Come on boy I say, come on boy. But he keeps barking, barking, barking.'

I stop counting. The old man steps back.

'You made the dog bark Dad, she says, you made him bark.' His finger wags in time with the story. 'I don't know how you did it but you used some signal to make the dog bark.'

The dog watches the old man.

'Anyways we walk down to the sheep, the wind flippin' and flappin' at me hat. You'll find this hat much cooler than your old one she says. Course'll be cooler I thinks. I'll fly away in this wind up into the heavens amongst them clouds.' One finger points upwards. 'But I don't say nothin.'

I laugh out loud again and the dog thumps his tail on the floor.

'Anyways we was walkin near the dam and dunno how it happened cos I had the bead up tight under me chin but me hat takes orf. Flies through the air like a bird.' he pauses. 'Dad, she bellows, Dad, then she takes orf after me hat.'

I laugh as he laughs at the memory.

'Come on Dad she calls, beckonin' me to follow. Can't, I yells. Have to stay in the shade now me hat's gone, to keep me face and neck shaded like ya said. I sat down with dog under a tree.'

He sits on a chair. The dog moves beside him.

'She comes back. Send the dog into the dam she said, it's in the dam. There's me hat swimmin'away in the middle of the dam.'

His hands wave circles in the air.

'Swimmin like a little boat in the wind. Now me dog likes a swim. Hot day and he heads off for a swim without bein' told. But not this day. Nope, sits on the bank, and watches me hat swimming roun' and roun' and roun'.'

The dog sits up, tail thumping the floor.

'Go on dog she says, go get the hat. But dog here just lies there lookin' at me. Dad, she says, make him get the hat. Can't, I say, dog is gettin' old, like me, some days he don't want to do things.'

The money is silent.

'I'm not leaving the hat floating in the dam she says. It's a perfectly good hat.

Well it is a hot day. Me bald 'head is stingin' in the sun so I pulls me old hat from me pocket and puts it on me 'ead.'

He demonstrates the process.

'Dad, she screams, you planned this, carrying that old thing in your pocket. Just ready for emergencies I say. Then she starts to laugh. Just like her Mum, can't stay mad fer long. But she weren't lookin' at me, she's starin' at the dam. There's me hat swimmin' aroun' in the dam with two willy wagtails sittin' on it, havin' a little sail like two la de das out on the river. Orf goes the dog. Splash into the dam, the two birds take off and whats the dog do?'

He looks down at his beloved friend.

'Whats the dog do? Leaves the hat swimmin' in the dam. Comes back then shakes himself over us both.'

Thump, thump, thump goes the dog's tail.

'Heard her on the phone later that night tellin' me son-in-law the story. I could have died laughing she told him, could have died laughing. Worse ways to die than laughin' I thought, worse ways to die. Good bloke, me son-in-law, good bloke. How's the countin' goin' sonny? You've slowed up a bit there.'

I tip the last from the tin.

'Well, whadya know, a farthing. Didn' know I'd been savin' that long.' He fishes the tiny coin from the pile.

'I've finished now.'

'Good job sonny, good job. Neat little piles there. How much?'

I tell him the figure.

He grins, lifts his hat, rubs his head and replaces the hat.

'That much.'

I nod.

He grins again.

'Now, if you'll just give me your full name and account number.'

'Crikey sonny I ain't got one a' those. Just give me yer biggest notes, that'll do me. Like I said the last bloke wanted to charge me fer countin' me money, unless I opened one a' them. Ain't gonna be bullied like that. Just yer biggest notes sonny and me 'n dog'll be on our way. Yer a decent bloke sonny and thanks fer yer time.'

Bay of Fires
The Gardens – Tasmania
Maree Silver

White beaches hug bays
outlined by granite outcrops,
giant marbles,
sandblasted,
flamed red by lichen.

A remote settlement clings here
at road's end.

Fishermen check cray-pots
anchored to long lines
stretching across the waves.

Boats scribble messages
in their motored wake.

Sea birds take flight
swirl and dip.

Clouds spiral and curl
into sapphire sky.

The velvet wind sighs
an ancient hymn.

The Right Direction

Mary Jones

Recently I caught the middle of an item on radio. It was an interview with an actor and a director, and I happened to tune in at the moment when the interviewer was asking them what Blocking is. The answers of both actor and director were a revelation, and so far away from most of my own experience that I felt like talking back at the radio to provide some alternative thoughts, on blocking in particular and directing in general.

'Blocking' is the process, which usually comes right at the beginning of the rehearsal schedule, of working out all the moves and positioning of all the actors. It includes entrances and exits, and interactions with furniture and props. It's often worked out in advance by the director, but usually changes after input from the cast in early rehearsals.

The response from the actor to the radio interviewer's question was revealing. He defined blocking as the process of making sure he was centre stage to deliver his lines, and to make sure other actors didn't 'upstage' him. (Upstaging is basically getting between an actor and the audience). He insisted that other actors always had to be watched out for, because they were all just out to get glory for themselves. He prided himself on his ability to grab and keep his central position.

I shuddered at this – I've worked with actors like him, and it was never a happy experience. I waited for the director to reply and redress the balance a bit. To my astonishment, she agreed with him. She said she saw it as her job to make sure the important bits of the text were delivered from the position that made them clearest to the audience, and she implied that that was always centre front. This was one of the points where I had to suppress the urge to shout at the radio.

The view that speech can only be intelligible if delivered from front centre stage is a very old-fashioned and restrictive one. It goes with the old instruction 'never turn your back on the audience', which is equally outdated. In these days of microphones and amplification, an actor can be heard from anywhere, on stage or off. In fact, even without microphones a competent actor should be able to project his voice from any position.

It was a short interview piece, so there was no further discussion, and the programme moved on to other items. It was one of those programmes that introduce guests at the beginning of an interview but don't repeat the information at the end, so I never got their names. I was left trying to imagine what a production involving the two of them might look like; a cast standing in a straight line at the back of the stage, perhaps, with actors stepping forward to deliver speeches one after the other. I've been to a few productions like that – but never stayed after the interval.

At the other end of the scale, I've been to a stunning stage production based on the David Niven film 'A Matter of Life and Death'. The main actor appeared in a small cage at the top of a high scaffolding structure, in front of which four actresses in nurse's uniforms lay on their backs pedalling bicycles held in the air above them, and the front of the stage was filled with buckets with flames coming out of them. Most audience members had a few moments of total bewilderment, before the magical realisation of what the whole thing really was – a pilot in the cockpit of a stricken Lancaster bomber, the bicycle wheels forming the propellers and the buckets the fire in the engines. Now THAT was blocking! And I bet nobody in that company worried about being upstaged, either. Interestingly, one of the London theatre reviewers gave that production a vicious slamming because of its unconventionality, and started a wide-ranging controversy about the merits of modern approaches to live theatre. Perhaps the critic would have preferred one of the 'front centre stage' productions my unknown radio friends were advocating.

***

The full purpose of blocking has always included giving the audience interesting visual experiences; it's to do with grouping actors when they're still and giving them believable actions when they're moving. It can also be used to manipulate and direct the audience's attention. For instance, in 'The Ghost Train', there's a scene where the station-master is telling a ghostly tale to a group of passengers. If the direction includes grouping all the passengers around him at one side of the stage and subtly and gradually altering the lighting so that it fades slightly everywhere else, the attention of the audience is focused so strongly on the tale-telling that their shock is palpable when the shutter on the ticket office on the other side of the stage suddenly falls with a crash at an appropriate point in the tale. Scattering the actors across the stage would not make the moment nearly as effective.

The size of the cast doesn't matter; blocking is just as important for a monologue as for a large-cast production. When it's done badly, it shows – a single actor given no movements at all is as frustrating for the audience as a large cast milling about in total chaos. Done well, it doesn't show at all; a perfect example of the general artistic truth that true professional craftsmanship makes things look easy when they're not.

It doesn't always work out well, especially when it comes to touring productions, where different theatres have different dimensions and audience sight-lines. I've been at a production of 'Hamlet' where nobody had bothered to check the sight-lines from the upper balcony. In the gravedigger scene, the whole top layer of the audience could see straight down through the trapdoor used for the grave, and we were treated to the sight of one of the stage crew sitting on a chair reading the newspaper, which didn't exactly help the suspension of disbelief.

Even the Royal Shakespeare Company can't be relied on to get it right every time. Playing Prospero in 'The Tempest' in 2006, Patrick Stewart was completely invisible from the balcony for the whole of his first long scene with Miranda, because they were both sitting down at the very front edge of the stage. People in the front row of the balcony were standing and leaning out over the safety rail to try to catch a glimpse of the main actor. We got an apology and a refund, but were still surprised that it had happened at all. It was probably because the production had transferred from a huge Broadway theatre and the set was massive – it didn't really fit the stage in London, and nobody had realised that some of the moves needed to be re-thought. So even the top professionals can be caught out sometimes.

***

The joy of live theatre is that it can be totally realistic or totally abstract or any point in between, so long as it creates a world the audience can believe in. This creation is shared between writer, director, actors and technical crew. In an ideal world, the whole team works together and everyone's input is valued, and somehow the whole becomes much more than the sum of its parts and takes on a magical life of its own.

Another joy is that the magic can happen at any level, including the amateur. Amateurs are often dismissed by the ignorant as always inferior to professionals, and it's true that the very best professional productions set a standard that amateurs probably can't reach. But they can come pretty close. I've been to plenty of productions by amateur companies and by schools that have moved me to tears or laughter or sometimes both together. I've also sat through plenty of professional productions that have bored me rigid. It's true that at the bottom end of the scale professionals simply couldn't get away with the awful depths plumbed by the worst amateur offerings. But a jaded professional cast in a matinee towards the end of a very long run can sometimes seem nearly as bad. There's actually a lot of overlap between amateurs and professionals in the middle of the scale, and the best professional actors and directors are usually generous enough to acknowledge the talents of their unpaid comrades-in-arms. After all, to struggle to establish a career in the theatre, or to give up precious leisure time to attend amateur rehearsals, both require dedication and passion – nobody's in it for the money.

But when it all goes right, there are moments that are sheer magic, and then nothing else in the world matches the buzz you get. When you hear an audience suddenly go quiet in that way that tells you they're really hooked, the tingle goes down your spine. If you're an actor, perhaps you react with another character on stage in a way that's never happened before in rehearsals, and it suddenly opens up wonderful new possibilities. If you're a director, you watch a performance growing and taking on a life of its own and you know you started it off. If you're a writer, you hear an audience laugh at a line, when you weren't quite sure whether it was funny enough, and you think 'Yes!' Sometimes they're quite small and fleeting moments, sometimes they're sustained and overwhelming. But they all come from making connections between people, and they're all amazing, and that's what live theatre is all about.

I can't help feeling sorry for my two overheard radio expounders of the art of blocking – they're missing out on so much.

This article won 1st prize in the 2016 Queensland Fellowship of Australian Writers Literary Awards article competition.

The Sequel to Happily Ever After

Judith Green

One sunny morning, three policemen stride up to the back door of the newly decorated house of the woodcutter, and his two children, Hansel and Gretel. Pounding on the door with their fists, they shout, 'Woodcutter, woodcutter, please let us in'.

The woodcutter is a little concerned with all the pounding and shouting. Are these three men really policemen?

'No, I won't let you in, not by the hair of my chinney chin chin,' the woodcutter shouts back.

'Then we'll huff, and we'll puff, and blow your house in,' the policemen respond.

'Go ahead,' the woodcutter laughs, very relieved. 'It won't work anyway. You're in the wrong story.'

'Damn,' they mutter, (well, they said worse than that, but this **is** based on a story for children), and leave.

One sunny morning, several weeks later, three policemen stride up to the back door of the newly decorated house of the woodcutter, and his two children, Hansel and Gretel. Pounding on the door with their fists, they shout, 'Woodcutter, woodcutter, please let us in.'

The woodcutter is a little concerned with all the pounding and shouting. Are these three men really policemen?

Someone's hit the replay button, he mutters to himself, before shouting back, 'No, I won't let you in, not by the hair of my chinney chin chin.'

'We've come about your children, Hansel and Gretel.' A pause. 'We're investigating the suspicious death of the old woman who lived in the gingerbread house in the woods.' Another pause. 'And the theft of her jewels. We just need to ask some questions, that's all.'

'There's lots of woodcutters in this forest,' the woodcutter shouts back. 'With all these trees to cut down we're a dime a dozen. We're all wood cutters, but we do have names, you know. Call me by name, so I know it's really me you want to talk to, and I'll open the door.'

Silence. Muttering.

'Rumplestiltskin.'

'Wrong story.'

'Damn,' they mutter, (well, their language was even worse than last time, but this **is** based on a story for children) and leave.

The woodcutter is deeply concerned. His children have a right to protect themselves, especially when a wicked old witch threatens to cook them and eat them. But he's been hearing rumours. Little Red Riding Hood and her Grandmother are facing animal cruelty charges. They've gone into hiding they are so afraid of what might happen. Cinderella is distraught. Something about the charming prince, charming a few too many chambermaids. Snow White's reputation is in tatters due to her living arrangements, and the three little pigs are being investigated by the local council for not complying with building regulations.

Enough to drive a man to drink, the woodcutter mutters to himself, looking out of his window in a melancholy manner. *Whatever happened to the good old days of happily ever after?*

'Hello. Care to join my band of merry men,' a voice calls from the treetops.

'Who are you?'

'I'm Robin Hood. I rob from the rich to give to the poor. Care to join us?'

'I've never heard of you. Do you get to live happily ever after?'

'Are you kidding! That only happens in fairytales!'

'Doesn't anyone live happily ever after anymore?

'No one ever did. Like I said, it just happened in fairytales. Are you joining us or not?'

'I'm coming,' says the woodcutter. 'Better than fronting those three policemen who keep pounding on my door.'

'We'll tell him about the Sheriff of Nottingham tomorrow,' Robin Hood whispers to Little John, as the woodcutter calls his children to pack their bags and come with him. Little John nods, smiling in agreement. A smile so broad, Robin Hood can see what big teeth he has.

'The Sequel to Happily Ever After' *was Commended in The Best of Times Short Story Competition #22*

Touching Paris

Maribel Steel

'I'm hungry, Mum,' our son reminds us as we move briskly past the scent of pain-au-chocolat drifting in the Parisian air. From the moment we leave Charles de Gaulle airport, it is hard to ignore the fragrance of this enchanting city.

Driven by excitement, we make our way to our friends' apartment in the 15th Arrondissement. I hear pairs of women trot by on clickety heels, and imagine them clutching chic designer handbags by Dior, Chanel or Yves Saint Laurent. Metres away, freshly percolated coffee catches in the warm summer breeze like an intoxicating spell, enchanting Harry and me towards the nearest café. Waiters in white aprons wave their hands like wands to produce a ready-made table for three.

'Madame? Monsieur?'

Harry and I pause, eyeing each other, then throw the waiter a broad smile. 'Pardon.' We have to stride on. Our teenage son grunts, 'How much further?' weary after the twenty-four-hour trek from our Melbourne home. He pulls our two suitcases gallantly as Harry smartens the pace, propelling me onwards.

'Another five blocks.'

We continue our trek in silence, tormented by delicious aromas, eager to arrive at our destination. We walk three abreast, me in the middle sweeping the ground with my long white cane as I trot to keep up. With only peripheral vision, I use the contrast of a cornflower-blue sky to trace the dark outlines of Parisian architecture, making my pace slow temporarily as I trail behind my sighted guides who pull me along like a child looking back at a toy shop. My heart desires to reach out and touch the ornate wrought-iron gates of a churchyard, or stop to run my hands through a clump of French geranium bushes.

'Hey guys, let me touch something?'

'STOP!' commands Harry and our trio pulls up sharp. We stand with a throng of bodies at a busy kerb, waiting for a gap in the traffic. My 'minders' move in close and hold my hand from either side as we meld into one neat package. My ears prick up to the sounds of manic traffic zooming past. Crazy drivers on motor-bikes turn over their engines as if to impress the crowd. Speeding scooters toot in a cacophony of horns; their two-stroke machines zip past like dare-devils as they weave between pedestrians, concrete bollards and the heavy flow of traffic.

My nose begins to twitch as I inhale the choking tones of 'eau de petrol'. The chimes of a church bell ring out as we near the apartment on Boulevard Lefèvre, carrying our prayers that Niquette and Didier are expecting us to arrive soon.

'I think this is it,' says Harry, as we arrive at our destination. He leans against a tall iron fence to look at a creased street map. Mike pulls up sharp, letting the two suitcases stand to attention by themselves.

'How do we get in?'

'Try the gate.'

'It's locked.'

'Damn. No battery either.' Harry sighs, putting his phone back in to his pocket.

What? I force together the carbon fibre pieces of my white cane as it collapses into a compact bundle tied by the extended elastic. Our friends are up there, on the third floor of their apartment, blissfully unaware that their friends from Australia have arrived. Jetlag is making us begin to wilt like parched flowers in the summer sun. Mike explores the perimeter of the sand-stone building, hoping to slither through a space in the iron-picket fence and unlock the gate from the garden side.

'What the heck are we going to do now?' I ask, regretting we have walked past so many delightful cafes in an exhaustive effort to arrive.

'Wait here, I guess.' Harry looks up at the windows on the top floor, massaging the sides of his temples. My feet lash out at the ground with dusty shoes, hoping to find a small stone we can try flinging at one of the top windows. Just as we begin to feel jetlag kick in with the boot of complete fatigue, the front door to the building is flung open. As if stung by a biting insect, Harry leaps up to call through the bars of the gate.

'Excusez moi, Monsieur...,' and asks if the man who has walked out of the front door could be so kind as to let us in? One pull of the buttress iron gate, and with several smiles and our copious replies of merci, Harry holds the fortress door open briefly as we scramble to drag our suitcases up the steps with renewed vigour.

'Ah, bonjour mes amis, bonjour!' Niquette hugs us each in turn, surprised to see three silhouettes crowding her doorway, with coats slung over arms, and flushed faces beaded with sweat after ascending the six LONG flights of stairs to their flat.

'Ow did you get 'ere? Oh, entrez, oui, oui,' she says, her eyes widening as the parade of suitcases trundles past. We squeeze through and create a baggage-jam in the narrow corridor. 'Mon Dieu. Didier,' she calls, 'zay ar 'ere!'

Over strong filtered coffee, and breakfast of freshly baked baguettes, creamy goat's cheese and a fresh green salad, Harry and I retrace the journey for our Parisian friends with theatrical flair.

'Well, d'accord. I sink we should go to the Jarden de Rodin,' Niquette announces. 'Your body-clock needs to feel 'appy with our Paris time. Voila.'

'Voila.' The three of us chant in unison, beaming smiles.

It is mid-May and our senses buzz with excitement to be strolling with Niquette, making our way through the streets of Paris to the Boulevard des Invalides. Niquette walks with me, arm in arm, chatting in half French, half English, giving Mike and Harry a well-deserved break from being my eyes and bodyguards. They walk independently a few metres ahead, and for the first time on our holiday I hear their male banter as they relax and become tourists, untethered from the responsibility of watching MY every step.

I sense the beauty of a place not with my eyes but with all my senses. My heart feels the silent reverie of my travel companions as if in a cloud of communal joy. In the Jardin de Rodin, I sense a different ambience as we stroll leisurely from the rose garden to follow gravel pathways leading to thriving shrubberies and shady nooks, along the path to the Garden of Orpheus.

On spotting one of Rodin's bronze torsos, Harry guides my hands to allow them to sweep gently across the fine and flowing contours of the art piece. I am enthralled and realise how touching with receptive hands gives me a deeper understanding of the artist. In Rodin's case, I can feel his intense love for nature and ancient mythology shaped into the folds of his marble and bronze statues.

Mike's tummy-clock tells us it is time to move on. As we make our way home with Niquette, our pace is noticeably slower as jetlag and Parisian life collide into a memory of our first day in fragrant Paris.

***

The following morning, I tiptoe to the kitchen and Niquette makes me a cup of coffee – a morning ritual I can't do without – while Harry and Mike steal half an hour more sleep. The apartment, with its narrow corridor, somehow fits in several shelves bulging with books and knick knacks. There are musical instruments from around the world, and Didier's intriguing collection of over two hundred spinning tops.

Harry and Mike appear in the doorway of the tiny kitchen. Niquette and I shift along the small bench seat. I smile, knowing that the smell of freshly baked croissants has caught Mike's attention. He is unusually chirpy for this time of morning.

Day 2; and we head off to join the thousands of adventurers in the center of Paris. Are we heading for the iconic Eiffel Tower or perhaps Notre Dame, the Louvre or a walk by the Seine? It doesn't seem to matter – we are in Paris!

I skip over metal grates in the pavement, hoping my white cane doesn't snag, and grip Harry's palm tighter, right hand thrashing the cane from side to side, while calling over my shoulder on regular intervals to reassure myself that our teenage son hasn't drowned in the rapids of Parisian bodies.

The trapped air of the underground is distinctive yet difficult to describe. Currents of air race through draughty tunnels smelling like a mixture of overheated metal, warm newspaper dyes and sweet chewing-gum – with not a trace of fresh oxygen until we begin to ascend the steps towards the street exit.

One of my travel buddies pushes me through the metal barricade and has to time the swiping of my ticket perfectly in order for me to get through. Brief panic subsides once we regroup on the other side.

'Where are we going?' I ask.

'To the mobile phone shop.'

As we weave in and out of pedestrian traffic, I am keen to know what shops we are passing, in case I can dive in for a fragrant souvenir or two. My male companions are not as keen on retail therapy as I am, and I sense a conspiracy when I ask, 'What shop is that?' Convenient deafness. No reply. We march onwards. 'Hello? What shop is *THAT*?' Knowing my number one dislike for seafood of any kind and being acutely aware of my love to touch anything given the chance, males one and two say in stereo, 'A fish shop.'

'Come on, guys, there can't be that many fish shops in Paris?'

'Yes there can.'

My sighted guides pick up pace and escort me neatly past pretty somethings in shop windows along the streets of Paris.

'Look! What's that shiny thing in the window?' I persist.

'Fish.'

'Don't be ridiculous. I don't believe you. Smells like Chanel to me.'

'Yep. Chanel for fish,' says Harry, and we keep striding onwards to the mobile phone shop.

Pretty soon, we are eating again. Niquette joins us for a soft goat's cheese salad in Le Jardin de Luxemburg. This 23 hectare garden has a small round lake, and in the southern section there is a honey-producing apiary in the urban orchard. We follow a narrow pavement outside the garden to hunt down a Cubist museum, where Zadkine (a Russian artist) worked and lived between 1890 and 1967.

The enclosed courtyard among soft green plants is unexpectedly peaceful here in the heart of Paris. Our quartet moves inside the compact gallery and I utter to waiting staff a new French phrase Niquette has rehearsed with me along the way. I wave my long white wand and with fluttering eyelashes, I announce, 'Bonjour Madame. Je suis malvoyante.' (Hello, Madame. I am vision-impaired).

She glances at the white cane. 'Oh. I understand', she replies in English. 'You may go in to the gallery for free, Madame.' The others pay their fees and as we turn to enter the gallery she calls after us, 'Madame? You may touch the sculptures if you are very careful with them. But only you, d'accord?'

'D'accord,' replies Niquette. 'Merci beaucoup, Madame,' smiling broadly as we walk arm in arm through the narrow door. 'Eh? Voila!'

I am overwhelmed with joy – touch the artwork? This is such a rare treat. What I manage to see takes my breath away: what I

manage to touch enlivens the seeing. And on this day, I truly see
Zadkine's sculptures of ebony, bronze, stone and carved wood
through dancing eyes at the edges of my fingertips.

Sixth Sense

Marguerite Kisvardai

I have been here before, in the waft vista sound zest caress of life.
Newly mown grass, a sharp sweet nutty scent.
High among stringybark branches a honeyeater's harsh call
breaks open a shell of silence.

Bitter yellow gleam of wild mushrooms
beckons along paths between tangled shrubs,
furrow of track, scratch of twigs,
quiver under skin.

Closer to the park fence endless noise of traffic
filters through trees,
passes in streams and clumps,
a long cry slicing my thoughts.

I turn away to plunge through melaleucas, touch
a papery trunk, taste a leaf, search again
for a memory of love, feel once more the throb
of pain and loss, find a moment of re-discovery.

Ego Tripper
Errol Broome

To write about myself is something of an ego-trip. To talk about myself is even eggier.

Yet I do it often enough. Each request to speak at schools or libraries tests my resolve to steer away from I ... I ... I. For reasons that still cause prickles of embarrassment, I realise I've been invited to talk about myself. Tell them how you go about writing ... where you get your ideas ... how you became an author.

I tell them that my first story was published when I was nine years old. It was about a cat that became lost in a forest and practised climbing trees till it was rescued miraculously by its owner – me! I remember my mother and grandmother, vocal in their surprise and joy, and my own matter-of-fact acceptance that this was what happened when you wrote a story. It got published. Ha, you live and learn!

What I don't always tell them is that my course was shaped the day I was born and my mother called me Errol Carew Moss, rather a burden for a girl. 'With a name like that,' said the doctor, 'she should write a book.' I grew up hearing this story and believing I would become a journalist, though I wasn't at all sure of a journalist's role.

I did become a journalist and learned a lot about writing clearly. They were good teachers, my bosses on The West Australian. Sometimes I talk about those newspaper days; how I began my working life on Australia Day 1958. Starting my career on a public holiday gives a fair indication of the life of a writer.

I spent many hours at law courts and airport interviews, and stopped thinking I would write a book. But years later, when my main acts of creation were over and our three sons were at school, I did sit down to write a book. It was called *Wrinkles*, about a grandmother who turned cartwheels, and published by William Collins in 1978. The second book took six years, but after the early nineties I averaged a book a year, all for children.

Then I think, this is too much about me. Please let me talk about other writers. I could tell them that Ernest Hemingway wrote the ending of *A Farewell to Arms* 39 times; that John Steinbeck sharpened pencils and wrote a letter to his editor before he started writing each day; that Alan Marshall made a cup of tea, checked the mailbox, stared out the window and wandered into the garden; that most of us find any excuse not to get started.

I might tell them that some authors know exactly what is going to happen before they sit down to write, and others have no idea. They just sit down and write. Some authors start with a story in mind and fit characters into the jigsaw of their plot. Others start with a character and let the story grow from the nature and actions of that character. A good writer gets inside the mind of the characters. Each character is an iceberg, and the author captain of the ship. The reader may see only the tip of that iceberg, but the ship's captain must know the 7/8 below the surface.

Oops! I'm beginning to sound like a teacher. Children have teachers five days a week, and I'm a visitor, not a teacher. This is the quandary: to try to help and instruct, or to talk about myself ... I ... I ... I. As something of a compromise, I carry with me some of my favourite beginnings. In teacherly mode, they're examples of good opening lines. Egotistically, they're pieces I wish I'd written myself. Whether teacher or ego-tripper, let me share with you a few of these.

***

'In the old brown house on the corner, a mile from the middle of the city, we ate bacon for breakfast every morning of our lives.' Helen Garner, *Monkey Grip*.

'My name is Herbert Badgery. I am a hundred and thirty-nine years old and something of a celebrity.' Peter Carey, *Illywhacker*.

'I was set down from the carrier's cart at the age of three; and there with a sense of bewilderment and terror my life in the village began.' Laurie Lee, *Cider with Rosie*.

'My name is Asher Lev, the Asher Lev about whom you have read in newspapers and magazines, about whom you talk so much at your dinner affairs and cocktail parties, the notorious and legendary Lev of the Brooklyn Crucifixion.' Chaim Potok, *My Name is Asher Lev*.

'We came on the wind of the carnival.' Joanne Harris, *Chocolat*.

And not forgetting Dickens' famous opening to *A Tale of Two Cities*.

Writers are always asked where we get our ideas, and after a few examples of my own I try to get group ideas flowing. The mind is a magic box, and the ideas are all in there. We only need to pull them out – and then it's called inspiration. For those who have trouble getting ideas out of the box, a few What Ifs can set the imagination soaring. And just when we have the story starting, a boy near the front asks which football team I follow!

The tips I hand out may work for some people and not others. Writing is very much a matter of style, and we all develop our own. What goes into my writing comes from my own experiences and feelings. Because I have not lived anyone else's life, I can pour only myself into the words. There are bits of me in all my books, in all my characters. Ben (*Fly with Me*) who did not want to go to school in his pyjamas, was reliving one of my persistent childhood nightmares. Fergus (*Bird Boy*) who jumped off the roof of the chicken shed, was also me. I am very much the shy Anke (*Dear Mr Sprouts*) who hides behind the letters she writes. It comes as a surprise to people who know me now to hear that

I managed to get through school without ever getting to my feet to speak. I am also Toby (*My Grandad Knew Phar Lap*) because I'm mad about the Phar Lap story, and I didn't have too much trouble turning myself into a mouse in the Magnus books.

So now, if you ask me to speak, you're going to get me. If we want a lecture on city buildings, we ask an architect or town planner; for a talk on global warming, a scientist; on barking dogs, a veterinarian. If we ask a writer, we'll get a host of personal experiences that lead into the pages of books. We tell children to write about what they know and, in the end, I can't pretend to be an authority on anything but myself. May I apologise now, once and for all?

Shooting Stars

Dulcie Stone

Third place in the Margaret Hazzard Short Story Award 2016

I saw a shooting star.
And then I saw another

His arm is heavy across my breast, his snoring loud in my ear. Is this it? Is this my life?

The moon, dying, leers through the window. He snorts, shudders, and resettles. I struggle, stealthily, to free myself. Don't wake him. Do not wake him. He won't talk about a child, nor do I. Only an idiot would bring a child into this mess. Do not wake him!

How in the name of God am I supposed to do today's work? Half my life nursing, in casualty, theatre, and the rest. Why? What's the point? I honestly believed. But every day's the same, slapping precision tools into anonymous gloved hands operating on anonymous lumps that will come to life again if we do it right. Will be dead if we do it wrong. Dead wrong.

He stirs. The leaden arm slips from my breast, flops onto the sweating sheet. Why does he sweat like he's just run a marathon? Because he damned near has. Every night, last thing, he's off down the beach for his evening swim. So what about me? What about us not talking any more? There's nothing to say. Not a damned thing that hasn't been said a zillion times already.

Stop it, Jess.

Why? It's the truth. Our truth. He swims at night. Me in the morning. He doesn't want children. Me... He sleeps at night, me never – almost never. He...

Stop? How? It's getting worse. It's getting harder. Every nightmare night it's getting harder. It's getting impossible. How do I drag my sleepless self through the pointless hours of each tomorrow? How do I escape the dead-weight arms across my breasts? Across my life?

Escape? Where to? And who the hell would understand my why? I can see, already, the thin lips and the slick eyes. Why would the fool leave? Top class nurse in top class job married to top class exec living in top class bay-side mansion.

My God! I've been around too long. I've seen the desperate women who fold under pressure. Or is it disenchantment that brings them low? Whatever. I will not add this disjointed self to that depressing horde. But how? Dear God, how?

Why tonight? Why is this night oddly worse? Many things, many, encapsulated in yesterday's six hour op that repaired yet another body irreparably abused by self indulgence.

I steal from the bed, easy and silent.

The track suit is ready, as though it knew it'd be working an early shift. I leave the silent house. Beautiful house perfectly designed, perfectly furnished, perfectly decorated, perfectly immaculate - perfectly pointless.

Bare foot, I cross the sand to the water's edge. Here the first Aborigines trod. The same sand? Science disagrees. Enough of science! To hell with clinical precision and careful knowledge. It's the same sand. My feet feel it.

The shimmering stars, defying daylight's oblivion, are pre-dawn brilliant. The sickle moon's silver reflection ribbons its seductive path across the dark water, thin and stark. Solid.

To tread that path. To set these tired feet and this empty heart onto that freedom road into the bay. To walk its silver mile and slip into its silent depths.

At the water's edge, the ripples curl across my feet. The same sand and the same sky and the same ripples that have comforted a thousand thousand years and more. A billion years and a zillion feet, gone, their fleeting prints drowned in the arrogant tides of the careless sea. I take the first step ...

And then, right then, the shooting star flares across my despairing sky; arching high and bright and free and splendid. Then falling. Falling. Fizzing into nothing. Just plain nothing.

There, and not there. But it was. On this momentous night, I have seen it.

So many shooting stars on so many empty nights and nobody sees. So why my shooting star? Is this my life? Am I the fizzing end of the dying star?

Is this what the star tells? The spectacular miracle of life, and the fleeting moment that is life. What about my fleeting moment? As quickly as the star shot through the pre-dawn sky so has my time sped.

I look up, hoping for more. I've got all I'm getting. No more shooting stars for me. I've seen all there is to see. Humility… Humility whispers what's so special that you should ask for more?

And the message is?

Make your own star.

I leave the sea and the freedom road of the moon's illusion. I go back to the sleeping house, farewell the smug snorer, and join the city bound traffic.

***

The CEO wheels his wheelchair into the office. 'Sister! How may I help you?'

'You can't,' I respond. 'I can help you.'

'How so?' The man with the ball-breaking job of running this model of excellence is unsettled.

'The Third World team you're trying to get off the ground?' I ask. 'How's it shaping up?'

'Not much joy there.' He grimaces, resigned to the inevitable. 'Too much risk. Not enough remuneration. Third world assignments are for the unattached idealist.'

'So why are you doing it?'

'PR, of course.' He unashamedly declares: 'Looks good. An exercise in window dressing.'

My heart drops.

'Cynical?' He's forthright. 'Of course. It goes with the job.'

Cynical I know.

He sets one elegant hand squarely on the desk. 'This discussion has a point?'

'I'm not sure…'

'Sit down, Sister.'

His chair is dead opposite, my face lit by the sun from the window at his back. His eyes, careful eyes, are in the shadow.

'This job.' He scans the perfect furniture in the perfect office. 'It's not from choice. I'd much prefer to be still in surgery. You knew that?'

'I'm sorry, Sir.'

'It's necessity, d'you see? Family obligations. It happens. Plus my health. D'you see?'

'No sir. I don't keep up.'

'Understood.' Back to business, he asks: 'Why are you here, Sister?'

'The overseas assignment. I might be interested.'

He shoves a sheaf of papers at me. 'Take these. Read them. Come back if you're still interested.'

Case dismissed.

I start to read.

'Not here.' He reaches for the telephone.

End of interview.

I fold the Third World papers, prepare to leave.

And then, right then, she comes into my life. The door opens and she rushes to fling herself at him, the careful man with the careful eyes.

'Daddy!' His daughter climbs onto the wheelchair, and hugs her father.

He abandons the telephone.

The child's sleek blonde mother apologises. 'I'm sorry, Alex. She got away from me. You're busy.'

'Not to worry,' I reassure her. 'I was on my way.'

But I'm not on my way any more. Their daughter is the most bewitching child I've ever seen. A dark-skinned cherub, her black eyes are dancing with the sheer joy of living. What's happening here?

'We're intruding.' The blonde is gracious. 'Trudy! Daddy is busy.'

Trudy kisses her father, and leaves with her mother.

The room is suddenly bereft. A light has gone out and we two are in darkness. My awakened mind sees the shooting star that lit the distant beach, the serendipitous star that brought me here.

I saw it, and I saw Trudy.

The CEO beckons me back. 'Sorry about that.'

'I was on my way.'

'I have a question, Sister. If I may?'

'Of course.'

'This overseas project, it's a huge step.' His eyes are warm. 'Are you unhappy here?'

'I'm frustrated. I feel at a dead-end. I feel...' Candour doesn't come easily.

'Go on.'

'To be honest,' I confide. 'I'm sick of wasting my life on self-indulgent fat cats.'

He laughs, a bubbling sound that is the echo of his daughter's joy.

'She's Aborigine.' I state the obvious. 'Trudy is Aborigine.'

'We met up north. The cyclone that condemned me to the wheelchair wiped out her family.'

'You worked up there?'

'My wife and I, yes. At an Inland Health Clinic. Until…' He pauses. 'Not to dwell, Sister. Enough to know that Trudy is afflicted with a terminal condition. She has a year at best.'

How to respond?

His strong jaw trembles. 'We were permitted to adopt her. We love her.'

'She loves you.'

'It should have been otherwise,' he mourns. 'Her condition was preventable.'

'I'm sorry.'

He recovers. 'I do understand your frustration, Sister.'

For the second time this fateful morning, humility whispers – how dare you ask for more?

Wrong! You've been gifted with a second star, the serendipitous radiance of his dying child.

And the message is?

Fate is giving you more.

He's waiting. Trudy's dad, with the sad eyes and the secret sorrow, is waiting. He believes there is another need and I, too, now agree.

'Please.' I return the papers of the distant Third World's need to his desk. 'Tell me about the Inland Health Clinic. Tell me about the children you had to leave.'

Download

Joan Katherine Webster

I regret to say I cannot address your meeting,
read at your gig… …

Like Shakespeare's sere, his yellow leaf,
this seer is a bit too close
to the end of the twig.

If the techno nerds
converted me to a URL
as they've done so well
with words, you could
download me in an appearance app.
Ask your ISP.

Customized in a Cookie,
popped in a Dropbox, digitally despatched,
I could be simulcast through the ether,
somatically shared,
scrolled down your page,
clicked, and unfold onto your stage.

Email me!

Pack me in a USB stick.
Transubstantiate me.
Process my particles through the cosmotic Cloud:
sinews beamed by satellite,
flesh Posted. Attached.
If my bones could be bounced
by hypertext, I could be Refreshed. I could WiFly!

I just don't travel so well
these days, far
by car.

(Don't forget to Save me.)

Soldiers' Dreams

Megan Wallens

Robert died. His only child, Jack, moved interstate just days later. I'd been Robert's live-in house-keeper and carer for two years. I planned to leave, too; with both men gone, my job was done. But as he departed, Jack gave me the key to the front bedroom, always kept locked. So I found myself staying with Robert's cold ghost for company on the lonely West Wyalong farm.

Jack's untreated depression had taken him to the dark edge of a personal abyss. While Robert lay dying in his angry seclusion, his son was chaotic, suicidal. Life's clock ticked towards the last hour. The house and farm filled with a despairing air that swayed with the men's unspoken pain. Then, Robert's breath stopped. With exquisite timing, Jack was released from his stalking demons by new medication, and his father passed into the eternal night. Like a newly unharnessed horse, Jack was set free to gallop towards the horizon of his dreams, away from the grieving sucked-dry paddocks of heartache.

'Thanks for looking after things here, Sal, and for what you did for Dad!' Briefly there was guarded love, then pain and grief bubbled out of him. The shutters came down over his navy-blue eyes – Robert's eyes.

'I'll miss you!' I replied untruthfully. He'd been a nightmare; I was glad to see him go. After pressing the damned key into my reluctant hand, he strode out to the ute yelling, 'There's something of his under the bed. It's all yours.' Then the bastard took off!

Under the bed, in the dusty shadows, lay a bundle wrapped in yellowed paper; it was bound with string, neatly tied in a spiral down the length. I hauled it out, saw the sealed envelope fixed underneath. The word read "Jack".

Unknowingly, I then crossed the Rubicon into unmapped Japanese territory. I untied the carefully structured knots, removed the envelope, unwrapped layers of paper. The samurai sword gleamed as I lifted it to the light. My fingers wandered over the wooden hilt, its perfect curved blade. Despite my ignorance, I could see the beautiful craftsmanship. Tied to it by thin dark threads were two raggedy cloth tags inscribed in ink with Japanese characters – one was of silk, the other calico.

There are fateful moments in our lives that change our destiny. As I opened Jack's envelope, I didn't know that this was mine. How I cursed Jack then. He'd deliberately not given me his contact number; wanted to be truly independent, so he said. Right when I'd planned to leave, he'd knowingly reneged on his filial responsibility, whatever it was, dumped his problem on me.

Written in Robert's fading hand, I read:

Jack. I was a major in the 11th Division of the Australian Army, based in Rabaul, New Guinea. I was on board HMS Glory on 6th September, 1945, when Japan's General Imamura surrendered to Australian forces. The Japanese soldiers were required to hand in their swords to be destroyed. There was a great pile of them. I watched as another young major, Japanese, placed his sword on the pile. Our eyes met and held. I saw tears run down his thin face. On a whim, I asked my aide to hand me that particular sword, and I kept it. I have no idea who that other major was, or of the sword's history.

I am deeply ashamed that it has taken this long for me to understand the effect of my lack of action, and my failure to attempt to reconcile with that Japanese major and his family. I know that I have prevented any possibility of healing to occur within myself, within you, within that family in Japan. I've been a great fool, probably damned to Hell.

I want you to return the sword to its original owners, if they can be traced. I want you to make amends for my lack of courage, apologise to them as I should've done.
I apologise to you, too, for my many failures.

Your father. Robert John Ainsworth. April 13th, 2013.

No 'I love you'. My heart lurched with grief as I grasped the darkness of Robert's bottled silent dying. And poor Jack had constantly borne the brunt of his father's angry pain without understanding any of it.

With help, I contacted the curator of the Army Museum at Lavarack Barracks in Townsville. He explained how to remove the sword's wooden hilt by knocking out a retaining dowel, and he waited on the phone while I did it. Then he asked what I could see. When I mentioned the inscriptions on the shaft's exposed surface, he became excited. 'Send me photos with supporting documentation; I'll see what I can find out!'

A month later, I received a formal letter from him. In part, it read: 'This is a sword of superb beauty. Fortunately, although worn, the ancient threads have held the inscribed cloth tags intact; if the tags had come adrift from their threads and been lost, we would have a difficult task. The tags provide the previous owner's name, rank and regiment, while the inscription on the shaft is that of the sword maker. Also, below the guard is a series of Chinese or Indian letter symbols, which have ancient religious significance. Initial research in Japan indicates that your unique sword was made towards the end of the Kamakura Period (1288 – 1333) by Masamume, a highly respected sword smith of the current Shogonate. It is believed that the rightful Family of the Sword is Kobayashi. However, it will be necessary either for you to travel to Japan with the sword and relevant paperwork (see list below), or for the Japanese Family of the Sword to come to Australia.'

Then, coincidentally, Jack called. It was three months since he'd gone. He sounded strong and clear. Taking a huge risk, acutely aware of his past mental fragility, I told him about Robert's letter, his agony over the sword, what I'd learnt since. I said I needed his help, asked if he would accompany me to Japan. 'Please, Jack! You owe me!' There was a long silence. Then, to my astonishment, he agreed. After that, he phoned me often. He was different now, energised and bubbly like a freshly poured beer, happy and loving his new life. And loving me, so he said.

Eighteen months after Robert's death, Jack and I finally took the sword home to Japan. Beforehand, the Japanese equivalent of Australia's Returned Servicemen's League had to pull together and verify the myriad details of the Kobayashi family. They needed to prove that Kobayashi was indeed The Family of the Sword. Following two meetings in Tokyo, where people were delightfully enthusiastic about our mission, we were directed to the west coast city of Niigata. The shinkanzen whipped us across Honshu through long mountain tunnels, east to west. Jack became increasingly agitated. He said he was simply nervous about his responsibility of handing over the sword. I wasn't so sure, anxiously held his trembling hand. 'Just one more day, Jack!'

At Niigata Station, we were met by our translator, and taken to the home of The Family of the Sword – the home that once belonged to Takao Kobayashi, major in the defeated Japanese armed forces, Rabaul, New Guinea, 1945. We were ushered inside by a bowing young woman, Yukiko. 'Please wait.' After long minutes, two solemn middle-aged men appeared. Silent, unsmiling in suits, they stood rigid before us. We all bowed and formal introductions followed. They were Takao's sons – Tadakatsu and Masakazu.

Jack suddenly dropped the sword we'd been so carefully protecting. He let out a gut-wrenching howl and staggered forward. The men instantly opened wide their arms, embraced him. It was like the bursting of a giant dam, as the inherited festering grief and sorrows for their fathers' separate but shared cruel worlds and wars overflowed. Their tears mingled on the fresh tatami matting; agonised cries of release reverberated well beyond the rice paper screens, and flew away together into a bright blue Japanese sky.

***

A year later, back in West Wyalong, I'm heavily pregnant with Robert Takao Ainsworth. The front bedroom is beautifully redecorated now, unrecognisable as the baby's nursery. And I've refurnished and painted Robert's room, ready for Takao's granddaughter, Yukiko. She's on her way to help me, to study English, cement the newly constructed bridge built between our families.

'I'm coming home. Picked up the pram.' Jack's just leaving town. On the mobile, his strong voice is full of hope and love, our shared future. And I'm standing in the silent hallway. The baby suddenly stirs and kicks against my side, as a chilly vapour comes from Robert's room, flows around me, down the hallway. Enveloping my body and unborn son with my arms, I watch as the front door softly opens, closes, and we farewell Robert's ghost for good.

"Summer grasses
All that remains
Of soldiers' dreams."
(Matsuo Basho 1644 – 1694)

NB. This story is partly based on true events.

The Society of Women Writers
Victoria Inc A0039632B

The Society provides:

- Monthly meeting and newsletter *Write Away*
- Specialist speakers
- Biannual journal: *Sparx*
- Postal workshops
- Publication of occasional anthologies
- Book launches
- Competitions and awards
- Interstate network with like-minded writers
- Literary seminars.

President
Blaise van Hecke
email: blaise@thebookchick.com.au

Membership secretary
Shirley Whiteway
email: shirleywhiteway@optusnet.com.au

To apply for membership
send the application form and cheque or money order to:

The Membership Secretary SWWVic Inc
78 Abbott Street
Sandringham
VIC 3191

SWW Vic aims to draw together women engaged in diverse writing genres.

Meet monthly on the last Friday of each month
(February–November inclusive)
4th Floor Ross House, 246-251 Flinders Lane, Melbourne VIC 3000 OR Library at the Dock, Victoria Harbour 12.00am–4.00pm

- Program includes workshops and/or guest speakers and critical readings
- Visitors and guests are welcome
- Tea/coffee available
- BYO lunch
- Entry fee $5

SWW Vic also offers

- Entry to competitions run by the society
- Possible inclusion in biannual anthology
- Workshops by correspondence: available to members isolated by geography/personal circumstance, designed for members who are unable to attend meetings and available to other members.

AWARDS
The opportunity to compete for biennial awards:

- The **Margaret Hazzard Perpetual Trophy** for a short story (open to members throughout Australia)
- The **Kathryn Purnell Award** for poetry (Victorian members only)
- **SWWV Biennial Literary Award** in various genres for women writers across Australia
- The **Nance Donkin Award** for a woman writer of books for children (inaugurated 2009)

MEMBERSHIP APPLICATION

SWW Vic Inc A0039632B

Name____

Address____

____Postcode____________

Phone (home)____

Phone (business hours) ____

Email ____

Writing interests: ____

____

Annual fee: (1 July–30 June) $45 (incl GST). For those who join after 1 January, the fee is $25 for the remainder of the financial year. Please add $10 for the year if joining a Postal Workshop.

Send this form with payment to the Membership Secretary. Annual membership is due and payable 30 June each year. For queries contact:

Membership Secretary
Shirley Whiteway
email: shirleywhiteway@optusnet.com.au

To apply for membership, send the application form and cheque or money order to:

The Membership Secetary SWWVic Inc
78 Abbott Street
Sandringham
Victoria 3191

https://www.facebook.com/societywomenwritersvic/

To find out more, visit the SWWV website:

www.swwvic.org.au